Literature written for young adults...

by young adults.

Allow yourself to be surprised.

Young Writers Anthology

Springing from Halls of Marble

Derek Koehl
Tavares Stephens
Rebecca Green
Nicole White
Editors

VerbalEyze Press
Atlanta, Georgia

Young Writers Anthology, Volume 2
Cover design by Derek Koehl
Senior editors: Derek Koehl and Tavares Stephens
ISBN: 978-0-9856451-1-3
Library of Congress Control Number: 2013938019

VerbalEyze Press books are available at special discounts for bulk purchases in the United States by corporations, institutions and other organizations.

For information, address VerbalEyze Press, 1376 Fairbanks Street SW, Atlanta, Georgia 30310.

VerbalEyze does not participate, endorse, or have any authority or responsibility concerning private correspondence between our authors and the public. All mail addressed to authors are forwarded, but the publisher cannot, unless specifically instructed by the author, give out an address or phone number.

VerbalEyze Press
A division of VerbalEyze, Inc.
www.verbaleyze.org/press

Table of Contents

Sarah Peden

L. M.

Michael Brown

Critical Reading Questions and Writing Exercises

Young Writers Anthology

Foreword

This edition of the *Young Writers Anthology* is a result of the vision that took shape four years ago. That vision—to foster, promote and support the development and professional growth of emerging young writers—became the guiding principle for everything we do at the VerbalEyze Writers Cooperative and through VerbalEyze Press. The *Young Writers Anthology* embodies two components of the VerbalEyze mission: one, to engage young people in and with creative writing and two, to provide talented young writers the opportunity to become published authors and learn the business aspects of being a professional writer.

Technology is transforming more than the mechanics of book publishing; we believe it enables a transformation of the very fabric of the publishing industry. VerbalEyze is working to bring the advantages of a new publishing approach to today's generation of young writers.

In addition to the craft of writing, we teach young people the business of writing and a revolutionary framework for writing and publishing that is fully cooperative. With the *Young Writers Anthology* and our innovative royalties model, we are enabling young writers to say, "I am my scholarship!"

We thank you for the support you have shown these young writers through the purchase of this anthology. *Springing from Halls of Marble* brings you some of the most outstanding poetry and short stories by college-age writers whose young years stand in contrast to the power of their words and the depth of their vision into the human condition.

Allow yourself to be surprised. We did.

The Editors

Note to Educators

"Before one can think critically, one must be able to think creatively."

Fellow educator,

Whether you are a public or private school teacher, a home school teacher, or youth worker, our goals are the same: to engage the creative capacity latent in all our children and teach them to harness that capacity to bring about change in their own lives and in the world around them. *Young Writers Anthology: Springing from Halls of Marble* is aligned with these objectives in two ways.

First and foremost, this anthology is literature written by young authors. Engagement with the creative qualities of literature is instrumental to the process of awakening creativity in students. I believe this engagement is strengthened by the perception of shared experiences and perspectives that occurs when a reader identifies with a writer.

Second, the editorial team at VerbalEyze Press contains several members who are also professional educators. For each selection in the anthology we have provided a critical reading question and a writing prompt, all aligned with the Common Core State Standards. The critical reading questions help focus students on core thematic and analytical aspects of the selections. The writing prompts variously challenge students to write in explanatory, analytic and creative modes as they respond to or reflect on central ideas and concepts within each selection.

We have invested our energies into making the *Young Writers Anthology* a reality for one simple reason: we believe in young writers and young people. We are encouraged that you share that belief.

Derek Koehl, M.Ed.

Caroline DeLuca

The Fish

My father and I are as different
as bells and birds, except for
a few passions he's passed on:
Mark Twain, travel, kayaking.

Two months after
we first waged war with Iraq,
and a week before his unemployment checks would end,
he decided the world was as enslaved
as it had ever been. Instead of a party,
he wanted me to come on a kayaking trip
that would retrace the escape of Huck Finn and Jim.

"Like a statement?" I asked.
"Like an escape," he corrected.
"We're not slaves."
"We're not free."
"I don't see how it'll help."
"You don't have to see. Will you come?"
I would.

On the river now, Dad says, "Don't splash,"
as my oar sprays drops of water at his shoulder.
A fresh breeze cools my brow. Cattails sway.

I drink the air, grip the oar. I can feel
new callus toughening my palms. We've been
on the river for five weeks.
We row, and eat cold deli sandwiches,
and stop ashore for sleep. I sit behind my father in our kayak
and stare at the constellations
of freckles on the bald globe
that is his head,
as if the patterns might clue me in
to what's beneath them.

Fish shimmy past. Birds dive at breakneck speed,
snapping beaks. The fish writhe
and flail.
Sometimes they escape, but mostly
they succumb.

Finally, after three bear sightings, thirty-eight sunsets,
twenty-two new freckles on Dad's head,
three kayak-tippings, and
one butterfly landing on my shoulder,
we reach the turning point.

Dad says, "We're here."
I ask, "How do you know?"
He says, "I know."
We sit, floating. The sky is so big, it might swallow us.

I watch him. His eyes are closed.
When he opens them,
he whispers, "Do you think we really have to go back?"
I look at him. My chest feels tight.
"Is there anywhere else to go?"

Dying Language

Inspired by the poetry of Erica Dawson

I was born, Mom says, with an old
heart, observing the world and its ways
with calm eyes, and a head that still plays
at imagining, and taking hold

of clues from strangers at
the market, for hoarding, scripting: Ring?
Wrinkles? Worries? Why? Wring
me out, I have some thoughts. They're tat-

-tooed on my scalp and back
in tribal symbols by Daddy Time,
relaying advice for the future. I'm
just flummoxed by mine. An anach-

ronistic and illusory piece
of Eve's flesh, I seem as though
I have it all together, alas no.
I'm not any closer to peace

or certainty than the rest
of the twentysomethings trying to ad-lib
their way through. I'm in the prime of my rib-
woman life and everything's a test;

and I can help my friends with theirs,
yet mine are mysteries in glyphs:
I can't explain my disconnection and what-ifs.
Like Mom's nightmares

of grappling with exams she'd fail
in foreign alphabets. No cues.
How do I deal with the tragedies in the news?
Daddy Time, are you frail

from watching millennia of pain?
Do you heal yourself? March on, cope?
Do you translate madness to hope?
Is there a way to make plain

to the world my language? I gab,
but none can fathom my wretched weariness,
or my 80's music-induced cheeriness,
or my gluttony for midnight confab.

Daddy, sometimes I'm so young –
trusting, dizzy, bold and boundless.
More often: tired, bewildered and groundless.
Can you read this fading tongue?

I Share Your Harvest

Once I made a promise to myself that I would stop getting upset over things that didn't concern me, but I find now that they're the main things I cry over: the tribulations of my friends and the deaths of characters in books I love, the ugliness of strangers' thoughts, how the sickly tree branches are battered by winter without mercy until they hang limp and defeated – and on the flip side I'm remembering all the things that sustain me that I cannot control – when people surprise me with their silliness, the thrill of a stellar play, a heat wave in February, and I think about that haiku, about the butterfly in the wind, half-flying, half-blown, and I think it is an artifice to say we are any different from that bug…we can cultivate happiness but there have to be seeds first; we need other gardeners to help us: our lives are commune farms, we sow collective crops and the joys and despairs of my friends or even strangers in the papers belong to me too, even when they hide them and hoard them and try not to be seen; our roots have tangled and it is too late…we cannot with sincerity say we are islands; and though I love you for your illusions, I love you more for the beating beast within you that must know they are not true - and so, know that I am with you; I am with you in the depths of your days and through every moment of your daily growing and dying and planting and reaping – day by day I collect your harvest along with my own, and you can feed on mine when you are hungry; I will try to sustain you with the memories and the snark and the pretty words I have watered and sang to and picked with the wind scraping my skin each day, and I know they will not be enough, but they are all I have to offer and I will offer all I have, and you think you are a Coney or an Alaska or a Maldive, but I promise you that you are landlocked, you are part of manifest destiny; I don't believe in fate but I do believe in inevitability, and I believe that since the day that the caveman first brought out a comrade and pointed to the sky and they watched together in bewilderment or wonder or tranquility, I believe that since then, it has been an ineluctable truth that for better or for bitterer, we are all of us tied together beneath the ground, and yes, sometimes a patch of hemlock or loathing sown by one will weaken us all, but we also keep each other alive with our stories and our senses and our promises that we so often fail to keep, and so it is manifest: here in our veins that after all are only roots within us, and can't you see them stretching outward, waiting to continue on a path in another's wrist?

 **Caroline DeLuca** is in her last year of the Writing Seminars B.A. program at Johns Hopkins University. She also teaches creative writing workshops to long-term patients in a Baltimore substance abuse recovery program. In her spare time she enjoys reading, theatre, spending time with family and friends, and taking walks at a decidedly New York pace.

She has been tinkering with words and stories ever since she wrote her first "book" at age five, which consisted of six pages and approximately thirty staples. Caroline is currently at work on a novel that will depart from the "more staples, better book" maxim of her earlier, more avant-garde creations, despite the notoriety it earned her among elementary school literati. This anthology is her first publication.

Leah Goodreau

Peter, Beloved

A mother stands in her kitchen, a howling child held to her chest. He ought to be toddling, eating, sleeping, learning. Instead he is small and uncomprehending, either silent or wailing. Once there were nannies, but they didn't last. Tonight she understands why; he's thrown up everything she tried to feed him, and his limbs buffet against her. The mother tries to sooth him, combing his thick, dark hair and swaying around the kitchen in an uncomplicated dance.

He snatches at her nurses' uniform, tears loose the top buttons. She has been so long holding him that she never changed out of her work clothes and now might barely have time to sew the buttons back on before her next shift. He screams as if his soul is burning, and the mother remembers a time when the piercing, ringing sound would bring tears to her eyes. His cries drown out the gentle *plink* of round buttons hitting the floor. She settles him on her hip; her shoulders creak and sag in relief. He is getting so heavy.

Kneeling, she sweeps her hand over the white linoleum. The child plunges his hands into her hair, dislodging pins and knocking her white cap askew. Her fingers clasp around his tiny wrists, hot with fever, and she looks in his rich brown eyes and hollers, "NO!" He screams as if possessed, but this is not a tantrum, something that can be disciplined. This is illness. Without her support, his head lolls back, uneven, blind eyes on the ceiling.

Unheard, Paula, small, straight and thin, stands in the

doorway. Her thick black hair has escaped its ties and sticks out like a dark, erratic halo. "Mom?"

The mother looks up, sighs, pushes up from the floor to face her daughter. "Go to bed, Paula."

"Should I take him?" her daughter offers. Though she is little and her brother growing, she never ignores a chance to be close to her Peter.

The mother's brow creases. "No," she says, "but you could pick up the buttons and bobby pins."

Paula nods and kneels down, her nightgown billowing around her knees.

The mother takes her boy into the living room and sits with him in the great upholstered chair. "I will do this, Peter," she whispers, her voice lost under his. "I can do this."

***

It is 1956. The mother sits alone in a great upholstered chair. The house is very quiet. She hasn't gone to work in a week. Eventually she will. Eventually it will stop feeling like betrayal and squandered effort to take care of other mothers' sick children.

She feels him still, pinning her legs, like the weight of an air-raid siren on the inner ear. Like the sirens, she can't tell if it is pain or fear or the ingrained, futile drive to stay alive that sent her ducking under tables. Back then, someone else fought and left her to her hiding. Now she hides again, behind tired limbs and aching eyes and a state school were someone else will pick up her battle.

She can't tell which weighs on her more, that strangers are taking care of her son or that she and her son are strangers.

***

The father drives his sleek Cadillac down a winding road. Their youngest girl sits beside him and strains to see out the window. Her Sunday dress, a little blue hand-me-down from the twins—its match hangs in the closet at home—crinkles in her restless hands. He parks the car on the side of the road.

"I'll be back," he tells the girl, but her attention is caught

26

on the tree-rimmed field of Black-eyed Susans off the roadside. He leaves the car unlocked and walks down the long drive through the woods, toward the gray building looming ahead. The receptionist greets him by name.

He would bring Anne Louise in if he could, but they don't allow children in these wards. Not as visitors. The walk down the corridors feels almost routine: the familiar cries of agony from behind half-closed doors, the familiar turning of his stomach. He is strong-willed. A veteran, a musician, a lawyer, he is a man who has been places and seen things. But these white-washed walls make his heart rage in his chest, make him feel small. It is not the deformed souls of twisted limb and body, the fuzzy-eyed and drooling, or even the wild howlers. It is the boys he sometimes sees in the halls, upright and walking, looking him in the eye. They might have cleft lips, the rich pink of their malformed gums split up to the nostril, or they might have bits of fleshy webbing between their fingers like frogs. What he wouldn't give to put Peter in their bodies.

Once her father is out of sight, Anne Louise slips from the car and dives in among the Black-eyed Susans. She kicks off her Mary-Janes and darts through the flowers. Running, dancing and turning her button nose to the wind, she brushes her stubby fingers over their petals.

The father sits by his son's bed, watches him squirm in a drug-induced sleep. He yelps and groans, round, guttural sounds like those of a puppy. The father rubs his thumb gently over the clammy hand twitching on the sheet. Peter jerks awake, but his father does not startle.

"Hello, Peter."

The head rolls toward him a second, then away. He likes to believe that Peter knows his name. The father talks in a low, steady voice, and gives Peter the news of the week. He tells him things which, even if Peter were a normal twelve-year-old, he could not have understood: law and investments, stocks and hierarchies. He cannot make himself believe that Peter listens.

The father walks back to his car. Anne-Louise, romping out in the field, sees him coming and runs for the fence. At the road's shoulder, she stops and puts her shoes on her dirty feet. Her fingers work so quickly, so surely. The father thinks of Peter's uncoordinated hands, the white fingernails always trimmed short so he can't scratch the staff during his episodes.

Anne-Louise climbs into the car, but he stands by his door and leans one elbow on the roof. Head bowed, he screws his eyes shut; his forehead crumples.

The father shakes it off. They drive home.

***

The mother is lying in bed when he comes in, shedding coat, shoes, and hat as he goes. She looks up from her lap, eyes narrow, and turns to the window. He settles on the side of the bed and heaves a sigh. From the basement, strains of Anne-Louise practicing scales on the old white piano float up to them.

After a long moment, the father looks at her. "I've been to see Peter."

"I'm aware."

"You never ask about him."

"Don't," she bites, her voice stale and brittle. "Don't you dare."

He sighs and lights a cigarette.

"Do you think I enjoy it?" She seems to speak through a sheet of water. "Sitting here in the damn quiet and peace while you go?"

"I can't stop going," he says, breathing out a cloud of smoke.

"I didn't ask you to stop. I just…" She chokes on a sob and throws her legs over the side of the bed, her back facing his. "How do you love him more? How can you go on when I can't?"

"This isn't about who loves Peter more," he says around puffs.

"No!" she yells, then slaps a hand over her face; her nose cracks with the force. "I should be taking care of my baby."

She crashes back to bed, arms squeezed tight to her body, gauzy nightgown fluttering to rest around her. The father watches her over his shoulder and drags on his cigarette as if it is oxygen. He stubs it out in the ashtray by the bed. As the last tendrils of smoke waft up, he leans back. His shoulders knock against the headboard, and he stretches one arm over her hair, cradling her head upside-down in the crook of his elbow.

"He's getting tall."

She closes her eyes, a thin stream creeping past her lashes. "Is he?"

"Mm-hm. Must be around five feet. And he has so much hair." He laughs, a hoarse, crusty sound. His fingers twitch for a cigarette. "Dark brown and soft, thick as wool. Like yours."

"Hn," she hums; the corners of her mouth quirk. Little trails of tears run down her temple, wet her hair. "Handsome?"

A ghost flashes before his eyes, the face of his son twisted like a bit of clay, all meaningless terror. A nurse with a needle appears. Then Peter's face goes slack, the mouth still a little open, and he sees the fine nose and thick, dark lashes laid on shallow cheeks.

"He's like an angel," he says, and leaves off *when he sleeps*.

She lifts her head a little, lets him slip his arm under her neck so he can get down on the pillows. Turning on her hip, she rests her head on his chest and runs her fingers over the crisp folds of his shirt.

"Tell me I'll see him in heaven."

The father shifts up on his elbow. "Now, don't ask that. You know I don't…"

"Please," she chokes; he feels his shirt dampening where her cheek rests. "I need to hear it. Please."

Heaving a great, rough-edged sigh, he settles back down and winds a calloused hand into her hair. It's nothing to him—

29

no truth to hold, no future he can convince himself to hope for. Meaningless. To her, it's everything, and though he can feel her tears sticking his shirt to his skin, it's like she's already gone. She's left him and the real Peter behind for an imaginary paradise.

"Yeah, sure. You'll see him there. And he'll be smiling all the time, and the first time he sees you he'll shout, 'Mama!' so loud God himself will cover his ears."

The mother drums on his ribs with her small fist, but she is laughing, laughing and crying and seeing it all like a vision in the sun.

"His beautiful smile."

***

The year is 1966. The limousine pulls up in front of the empty, pale house. Mechanically, the father clambers out and offers a hand to the mother. The twins come next, together, Beverly and Barbara. Though they have long since outgrown their mother's desire to put them in matching outfits, there is no denying the mirror-image of their black dresses, intertwined fingers, and downcast faces. Then Paula and her boyfriend step free, home from college for the occasion. Despite red and puffy eyes, the set of her strong brows and her unforgiving clutch on Roy's arm make her look about ready to hit something. Last comes Anne-Louise, subdued, playing absently with the end of her long single braid.

As the limousine slips away into the quiet suburban dusk, they stalk up the stairs to their door like soldiers marching toward a battle already lost. Paula tugs at Roy and nods toward his car in the driveway. He shrugs, digging his keys out of his pocket. They retreat; Paula grabs her little sister's shoulder.

"Come on, Ace, let's take a drive."

A smile flashes across Anne-Louise's face before she can stifle it. Paula and Roy each take one of her small hands, and they escape the house full of mourning for a little while. The parents pay them no mind but enter the house with the twins on their heels.

The mother disappears immediately into her bedroom,

ripping her flimsy black hat from her head as she goes; hat pins clink on the hardwood floor. Beverly and Barbara stay only long enough to look at their father, who stares at his children's little blackboard in the kitchen as if it were some foreign object. There are the names, painted in soft pastels across the top: Bevy, Barby, Paula, Peter, Anne.

The twins ghost away to their room. So quietly, so slowly, they help each other unbutton their black dresses and hang them up. Beverly stands looking into the closet as though the dresses will spring free and come at her; Barbara climbs onto her bed and rests her head against the wall. Beverly turns, takes a step toward her own bed, then looks to her sister. Barbara sighs, so soft, and lays her hand flat on the covers next to her. Her twin climbs in; they are too old for this, much too old, but still she leans into that shoulder that has always meant she would never be alone. Beverly cries for both of them, and Barbara comforts for both of them.

The father jerks from tailbone to shoulders when the doorbell rings. From the gray, fuzzy uniformity of absence, he crashes back into the kitchen, back to the aching in his feet and between his eyes. He considers ignoring the door—whether an early condolence offerer or some random bastard with bad timing, he is not in the mood to receive them. The bell rings out again, and he catches a flutter of shadow at the window. He thrusts the door open, *This is a bad time*, already forming on his lips, when he stops.

She stands on the tiny porch, worrying her purse in her hands. She looks up under the rim of her low-sitting cloche.

"I'm sorry, I just…" How can she convey what she saw from outside the family ring, standing with the lawyers from the firm? She has never seen such grief on his face, that strong and intelligent face with wide jaw and rapidly thinning hair. This is her boss, her mentor, her lover. How can she express what his mourning meant to her, how exquisite and terrible it was? How can she say she envies that pain?

"I just wondered if there was anything I could do for you."

He doesn't quite look at her, but slumps against the door frame under the weight of his own body. "If you could look over the Keimen case for me, I'd appreciate it."

The inside of her lip tastes coppery from gnawing. "Of course I will, but that wasn't... exactly what I meant."

He looks over his shoulder, but the hall is dark and quiet. "Not today. Thank you."

His dark eyes slide over her as if she is a mirage, shimmering toward nothing the harder he looks at her.

"I'll come back to the office as soon as I can."

"I'll... keep everything in order for you." She reaches out, face flushed with heat, and gives his clammy hand a squeeze. "Sorry."

"Yeah." He stands on the threshold as her heels click down the stairs but closes the door before she reaches her car.

***

Paula's window is down, wind whiffling through her short, thick hair. Roy strokes his beard as he drives. Between them, Anne-Louise feels flushed, even with the cool breeze. Paula spots a little shop off the roadside.

"Hey, Ace, you want some ice cream?"

"Sure," Anne-Louise chirps.

Roy pulls up next to the white plastic picnic table. They don't have much appetite. Anne takes a few bites from her little foam cup before watching the chocolate ice cream melt, smooth and shiny in the bowl of her plastic spoon. Roy chomps at his cone with the air of a man who does the only thing available to do. Paula's fists sit on the edge of the table like little grenades.

"I wonder if he ever did really know his name," she says into the silence. Roy gives her an inquisitive look while Anne buries her eyes deeper into the melting ice cream.

"Dad thought he did. I only got to visit him a few times, but I was never sure." She flexes her short fingers, her rings flashing in the light.

"Maybe he remembered it from before the meningitis set

32

in," Roy says. "Do you really want to talk about this now?"

"But what does that even mean?" Paula says, eyes fixed on the table. "He might have known his name. Just that, 'Peter,' just two syllables in a world full of noises that he could barely hear and didn't understand. He didn't even know what a name was. He couldn't tell between nurses screaming at him and Mom singing to him....

"So he knew his name. Maybe I could believe that.... But did he know what we meant when we said it?" Her voice is pitching like an under-tuned piano.

Anne takes a brave bite of soupy ice cream and risks a glance at Roy. He looks thoughtful. To Anne, Roy always looks thoughtful. He came from the land of college where Paula had gotten so many ideas and you were encouraged to write in your books. He leans over, so suddenly that Anne almost doesn't have time to demurely avert her eyes, and covers Paula's grimace with a kiss.

Paula closes her eyes, her forehead creasing as if preparing to cave in. She pushes into him in a way she usually wouldn't, not with her Ace around. His beard prickles her lips and chin and the sweet nuttiness of pistachio and waffle cone lingers in his mouth. Anne stands up to throw away her chocolate soup.

***

In the bedroom, he finds the mother leaning out the open window, a cigarette pinched between her fingers. Her black dress crinkles under her knees. Her eyes are red and weepy like infected wounds. She is stout and worn, puffing smoke; his eyes catch on the patches of white hair coming in at her temples.

"Come now," he croaks, all attempts at gentleness drowning in his rough throat, "Anne-Louise would be so disappointed."

She takes a pointed drag. There are no ashtrays anymore, not since Anne-Louise made a fuss about the cancer nonsense and hid them, so she lets the ash fall out the window.

"It's silly," she says.

"What is?" He asks because he knows she wants him to.

The end of her cigarette, with a flick of her wrist, sails out into the yard. "When I imagined him in heaven, I always imagined myself already there. Waiting for him."

It is silly—how could she have expected to outlive him?—but he figures it is only fear, the wish to not suffer this day's sorrow more than once. The father says nothing and unbuttons his vest.

There is more she could say, if she wanted to. Peter was not handsome, really, at least not in his coffin. She should have known better; his face had not developed quite right, from the meningitis. Oh, he had the thick eyelashes and dark hair, and his skin could be lovely were it not so waxy looking.

She wishes she could have seen Peter smile again, but she holds her tongue. Smiles must have been rare on those Sunday visits, and her own decision had kept her from them. The last smiles were the father's alone; she will not admit how she covets them. She takes the pack from her purse.

"Sharing?" the father asks, settling on the end of the bed.

She holds the pack toward him as she tugs the night stand drawer open for her matches. While she slips free her own cigarette, he takes the box and strikes a match with a scratch, the spurt of flame catching. She leans closer and lets him light her up.

Leah Goodreau
I'm a college student from New England living with four silly cats and an overabundance of paper. Most of that paper has been scrawled on, covered with sketches, lovingly forgotten at the bottom of my bag, or put in a very special place where I will never be able to find it.

My obsession is storytelling, however it can be done, but especially though books. One of the only ways I can engage with the past is to think of it as nonsensical, rambling story. When presented with dates and facts, my mind wants to make scenes. Writing based off my family, even those I never met who now survive only in anecdotes, makes me feel closer to my own history. I can love them like I love the characters of fiction.

Janelle Fine

Paper-Nymphs

inked
twitchings
across
my
page–
the
marks
of my
pen
where
I catch
myself
playing
in the
margins.
Not paying
any
attention
to you–
repeating

cubes,
making
water
waves
run,
pen-spirals
eat
delicate
four
legged
spiders,
now
scribbling
repeated
wings.
Tired of
drawing,
pretending
they
dance–
wish
they
would
breathe.

City Streets

Wheels asphalt pavement black pavement screeching pavement grey pavement—passing cars passing wheels thin and black—You pass the window riding on two wheels thin and black pavement black grey blue grey sky—pavement underneath sky blue grey pavement black bitter asphalt—bitter lungs she smokes—waiting for four wheels—to take her home.

Red Yellow Blue

Daddy tell me it's ok.
Yellow shirt to school–
and not know how to ride a bike.

To draw in the sand at recess–
I can't
run
tether ball
double-dutch
afraid to skin knees.

Red and yellow make orange
how to mix that shade–
the color of you.

How to smear paint across
be messy,
neatness is an art form.

You turn the pages
of your magazine
like a squirrel methodically
searching.

Tie my own shoe:
the bunny ears
cross and under.

How it was–
I want to tell you everything.

How I am–
Can I be a poet–
and breathe words into the world?

Bathtub

I get to the edge and begin descent.

One toe at a time,
dancing like skipped rocks
rippling the surface–
water's edge.

I slip my foot in,
line between water and skin bleed–
filling in the void between my legs,
creeping up my neck–
Completely under.

Janelle Fine is a poet and artist from Los Angeles. She found her love for being creative as early as preschool, where she began to draw and then started writing poetry in the third grade. She has had a love of words ever since she can remember. It has grown considerably since then and she self-published her first poetry anthology titled *Wildfibers* at the age of 18.

Janelle received an undergraduate degree from The Evergreen State College and is currently pursuing an MFA in poetry from The Jack Kerouac School at Naropa University. She is greatly inspired by Gertrude Stein and is interested in where the artist intersects the writer, painting with words. She brings visual imagery and the techniques of painting into her written work as much as possible.

Janelle is interested in combining the visual arts and poetics by creating handmade artist books. She is currently the founder and editor of an artist- and collaborative-based small press called Matchbook, with the goal in mind of bringing poetry and art to people's pockets. The idea behind the press is that matchboxes filled with poetry and art can transport creativity everywhere.

Shefali Srivastava

The Immortal Dreams

I fish my dreams in castles of sand
Built by naïve and gentle hands
Which know no languor, sorrow or pang
But yearning, hope and happy end.

I fish my dreams in nests on trees
Caressed by God and blowing breeze
Guarded by kindred and the leaves
Where warbles of joy never cease.

I fish my dreams in graves of soldiers
Built to commemorate their purpose
Where candles stand like sun in the sky
But never set even for a while.

Love Prayers

I build my chariot
On castles of music
And land in a nest
Where birds of love flourish

And I soar to God's place
Far above this world and hell
At his feet I offer their songs
He rejoices, He answers all.

I build my chariot
On castles of music
And land in a home of joy
Where mother sings a lullaby.

And I soar to God's place
Far above this world and hell
At his feet I offer her song
He rejoices, He answers all.

Fantasy

I fantasize a world
Where I surge
On the drops of spring
I listen to its heart beating

And then on my wings
I soar to palaces and places
Where people lend me ears, my dear
I convey his message to all who hear.

I fantasize a world
Where I enter
Into a saint's dwelling
Of words soft and caressing

And then back on my wings
I soar to palaces and places
Where people lend me ears, my dear
I convey his message to all who hear.

Memory Lane

Down the memory lane
Across the window pane
There's poured heavy rain
Of love, life, pleasure and pain.

Some stars in the sky are winking
Some cooing birds are fluttering
And we few among the crowd
Carve our names on pebbles lying.

Down the memory lane
Across the window pane
There's poured heavy rain
Of love, life, pleasure and pain.

Shefali Srivastava
Born in Lucknow, the Golden City of the East, I was brought up in Pantnagar, a town famous for having the first agricultural university of India on Land Grant Pattern, where I am currently pursuing my Bachelors in Agriculture. My name, 'Shefali' is another word for night flowering Jasmine, and like the same I attempt to charm my readers with fragrance of my words.

Georgia Googer

Hi Jaw-jaw

My grandma was in the kitchen humming along to her favorite opera, *Don Giovanni*. The butter aroma of another pound cake filled the house. Sitting in the adjacent hallway, I played with a petite doll. Made from a rough fabric, the poor thing was beginning to show signs of love and abuse. Anyone who peered around the edges would notice where the stuffing was just barely peeking through from all the long hours of tea parties. As the scent of cinnamon swirled around me, I asked my faithful toy if she wanted a small fake biscuit or petit-four.

"Dolly," I began, when I was promptly interrupted by the loud and mildly obnoxious peals of laughter erupting from the mouth of a two year old boy. My younger brother exploded through my special, very private, tea-party hallway on his beloved Tonka Riding Car. Cups and saucers scattering through the air were all too familiar to me. For far long I had tolerated his interruptions on my busy and precisely scheduled personal life, but that day was different. That day, my four-year-old self was going to make some changes.

Born June tenth in 1996, young James Henry started our now two-year bond of siblinghood off on the wrong foot. When he first came home from the hospital, I was keyed up. It was like a dream come true! In my toddler mind, I figured he would be sort of like a real life toy, unlike my aggravatingly unresponsive burlap Dolly. He would be something I could dress up, play with for a bit, and then put back in a crib where he would remain quiet and safe until our next play time.

These grand ideas of mine could not have been farther from the truth. After I almost dropped him off the couch the first time I held him, my parents deemed me a bit too young and irresponsible to be near him. As they removed him from my lap I saw him grinning. I tried to explain that he liked me and that he wanted to sit with me, but my parents would not listen. Instead of feeling torn by our untimely separation, the child started smiling wider! I knew in that moment that he was taunting my failure at my first opportunity to be a caring older sister.

As the next few years progressed, our relationship became more and more tested. I earnestly attempted to warn my parents about his terrible ways. I tried everything from waking baby Jim up from his naps so he would cry and they would hear how unreasonably loud he was, to dropping his bottle on the floor so they would notice what little care he had for his personal belongings. None of these plans worked though, and I was often punished for "bothering sweet baby Jimmy." After my usual scolding, I would receive a smug little smile from my brother, a signal that he knew I was in trouble and he was not. This became an agitating habit of his that he would use up until he was ten or eleven.

After two years of his tomfoolery, I knew something needed to change. My brother needed to learn that he was not in control here; I was. I was older, and therefore wiser, and he had to figure out that it was important to respect and follow the rules laid down by his elders. I loved him dearly, I truly did, but he obviously did not feel the same. Why else would he dedicate every waking moment to making me miserable? It seemed to me that the first step in mending our strained relationship was to remove him from my little play-time hallway. Maybe, he would finally begin to get the picture.

"Hi, Jimmy," I said to him as he was about to go blazing by me and Dolly.

"Hi Jaw-jaw," he replied. His inability to say my name was often thought to be very cute. Even I had to admit it was a tad adorable.

"Why are you riding your truck here?" I figured an innocent question was the best way to approach this family intervention.

"I like truck! I want truck go fast!"

"Jimmy, your truck is fast."

"Fast fast fast!"

I concluded that my solution to this whole ordeal was to find a new place where my brother could ride his truck and have it go faster. It was in this moment that I had one of the worst ideas of my life. Perhaps it was the overwhelming fragrance of cinnamon, or the rowdy cheers that spewed from the television as my father watched his Sunday afternoon football, but some external factor made my thought process go awry. I decided in that instant the obvious solution to all the mayhem was to convince my brother to ride his truck down the stairs. The staircase in question was about ten steps in total, covered in a slick carpet, and rather steep. All of these qualities would aid my brother in his endeavor to "go fast."

"Jimmy, come over here."

"Hi Jaw-jaw."

My brother came over to where I sat and rolled off of his truck, giggling the whole time. I grabbed his hand and positioned him in front of me, so we were both seated in a crisscross apple sauce manner. As we sat, I explained my idea. The words flowed out of my mouth quickly and convincingly. By the time I was finished his eyes were brimming with awe. It was like I could see his mind moving, considering the genius of what I told him. He jumped straight back onto his truck and placed it in front of the stairwell.

I stood up to watch my plan in action. With one enthusiastic push of his legs, Jimmy flung himself and his truck towards the stairs with an alarming velocity. The event happened swiftly. I stared as my brother bounced noisily down the stairs, his descent becoming faster and faster, until he reached the bottom with a loud crash. I could sense my father hearing the commotion and standing to see what was happening, but I didn't react. I was too busy hearing my heart stop as I gazed upon the results of my actions.

There are a few moments that everyone, young or old, can recognize as terrifying. Those frightening few seconds when you see someone, his mouth open wide, eyes shut tight, face turning red, no noise coming from him. In that brief bit of time, there is no distinguishing if you are witnessing an intense amount of pain or if an inexplicable supply of happiness. I saw my baby brother lying on the ground in front of our door. My heart beat so hard and violently I thought it was going to come out of my chest. I was aware of everything going on around me: my father about to run down to grab Jimmy; my grandma coming out of the kitchen to see what was happening.

None of it mattered. I stood still, too terrified to move. Had I killed Jimmy? Or was the next sound to come out of his mouth an eruption of laughter? This moment severely altered my perception of the world. Until then I had never considered the possibility that my actions could directly influence someone; let alone in a negative way. As I stared at my sibling, it all began to make sense. If I had not suggested he push his truck down the stairs he would not have done it. It was such a simple conclusion, but that did not hinder its significance. I was entirely responsible for this situation, and whatever was going to happen next was my fault.

The noise my brother made was one of joy.

Several hours later Jimmy and I sat coloring at our small table where all such craft activities were done. He had been thoroughly scolded by my father for his race down the stairwell. I, much to my surprise, went unnoticed during the exchange.

"Jaw-jaw, green."

My brother sniffed dolefully as he grabbed for a crayon near me. I stared as his face, still stained from his tears after my father had chastised him, and felt a twinge of guilt. Despite our differences, we were family, and I vowed never to allow anything bad to happen to him.

"Jaw-jaw blue."

 **Georgia Googer** has been writing short stories and poems since she was a child. Throughout the years she has won several essay contests, including the Laws of Life competition, and was featured in her high school's literary magazine. Outside of writing, she enjoys playing sports and can often be found outdoors. She is a flannel shirt enthusiast and loves both cooking and eating.

Georgia is currently an English major at Young Harris College and hopes to become a teacher so that she may one day share her passion for reading, writing, and learning with students.

Jolene Paternoster

Afternoon Lullaby

My child sits on a pink knit blanket
on my mother's full-sized bed
opening and closing her fists and mouth
to the rhythm of her need for me—
to the rhythm of a song I do not know.
But I move to it anyway, my terry-cloth robe,
the costume of my discontent, dragging too long
on the floor, and when I bend to pick her up
and place a mother's hand behind her head
and one around her waist, I am the one being lofted
feet above the ground. She cradles me straightjacket tight
against her robe, still warmed by my memory and rough
against my cheek, but still she doesn't feel the beat of my need,
how it begs her to take me in her arms and dance to it—
instead she places me back on the blanket.
She leaves me there and I sing myself to sleep.

Point Pleasant Beach in January

The gull's black tipped wings peek above the water,
bobbing metronomic in the wind.

On the shore, iced sand whips across my boots
and storm doors slam against their frames.

I came here because lately I've been
having trouble forgetting myself

and they all swore the ocean
would be a good distraction.

So I stare across the graying sea.
I take the prescribed walks.

I catch glimpses of my face
in closed-for-winter store displays,

and my thoughts drown out the echoes
of shut down Ferris wheels.

I am all consuming.
But the gulls—

I eye the gulls. One flies
overhead and drops

a fishtail from its mouth.
I eat the tail.

Anniversary Card: To My Mother

When I re-enter a room, he looks at me as if I am you
and you are twenty-two again and my curls are yours,
spilling out from under a crown of peonies, grazing the skin

under your knotted lace sleeves, and he loves you, like he did
when you were seventeen and you tried to flatten them
under tin cans of soup or a hot iron, and he loves you
like he did when I was born and you said she has her
father's dimple in her chin, but my father saw only you.

And when I visit my expired home, when he sees me
testing the posture of adulthood, strutting across the
oriental rugs with a coffee mug or the morning news,

I am you again, and the curtains are the ones you made
from old top sheets, moth-holey but thick enough to
block out the street-lights of Wallington, New Jersey,
heavy enough to hold the hot air in, where two lived in this
space meant for one and when he said, so, we'll get married,
you said, of course we will, and it was done.

When my father says goodbye to me, when I have to leave
because age has become distance and there is only so much
room left in the house, he is saying goodbye to you and you're

running late and haven't had enough coffee but this morning
the sheets look like gossamer and when he says good-bye
to you it's like he just remembered the reason he walked
into the room and he's found everything he needs and wants
to stay there, twenty-two, until the street-lights burn out.

My Grandmother Marie

You were doing laundry on the front porch
when it happened, plunging sweat soaked undershirts

into the metal tub, waves of soap foam splashing
past your elbows, darkening your sleeves.

When your father told you they found your brother's body,
you ran to lie in the imprint he left in the snow.

There you caught the cold, the one that lasted
all your life, the one I took from you when I was seventeen,

when I found you on your lawn, hallucinations
rattling your mind, when I took your frostbitten hand

and laid down next to you, you crying out his name,
me crying out yours.

Jolene Paternoster

Twenty-Nine Days More

I awaken when the false bamboo shades
start to leak morning across the shag rug, again,
and as always, revealing the glint of fallen coins
that I can't make seem worth picking up.

When I say I've stopped dreaming, I know
I mean that I've started forgetting my dreams
and that you, faraway and indisposed,
are thought of too quickly after waking,

and that present things, metallic and real
or quilted together from the fabric
of an idled subconscious, fall too from my mind.

Meanwhile strangers keep telling me
what glorious mornings we're having.
Meanwhile I've started bundling time,
days into phases to make them move quickly.

Yesterday morning I couldn't sleep. I sat
in the park at a picnic table. The goose I saw
folded its wings across its mud-racked chest
and tucked its beak in the seam they made.

It stayed with me like that all morning,
nestled into itself and squinting against
a sun gleaming blinding bright, and on
the wrong side of the country.

Sunday

I walk in late. I sit in the back
alone. Without my grandmother.

When she begged to die,
no one heard her.

Now, when I come here, I get
mad at God.

And I am afraid that she
is watching me from heaven

and knows that I'm not sure
that I believe.

Worse, I am afraid
that she was wrong

about the whole thing.
That she is simply gone,

like the water left in the baptismal font,
the water that evaporates

because no one uses it
to make the sign of the cross.

Junkyard

Broken metallic
modernity.

Aluminum pipes
strangle bikes.

Dolls'
heads.

Swing-
sets.

Brother, you would have liked
the upturned boats and ceiling fans,

the stereo whose wires
reach serpentine, and far,

and the crane,
a story high,

grabbing
plastic toys.

Jolene Paternoster

Each day
I have to see

the remnants of the years
you made yourself forget,

packed behind the garage door
that no one wants to shut—

where our old double stroller
rusts on the concrete floor,

where she hid that bag
of the things we couldn't let you have:

stained
steak knives,

shards of glass,

the day our father started sleeping
wrapped in your plaid quilt

at the foot of your bed
as though you might come home.

We could have found this place again.

Driven on a Tuesday afternoon.

Stolen a few
suitcases or

cracked doorknobs.
A standing clock.

Something we could have tinkered with,
something we could have fixed.

There were only hardwood floors
and hallway rugs between us then.

Brother I was a sister once and now I am nothing.

Jolene Paternoster currently lives in West Virginia, where she enjoys work as a freelance editor and publishing assistant. She majored in English and French at Skidmore College, and a portion of her senior project in poetry received a college-level Academy of American Poets award. Her work has appeared in Skidmore's magazines *Folio* and *Palimpsest*, in the online literary magazine *Vox Poetica*, and in print in *Barron's Magazine* and West Virginia's *Dominion Post*.

As Jolene grew more serious about poetry, she began to realize she most often draws inspiration from those closest to her—particularly her family. She is especially interested in the idea of heritage, and she intends to use poetry to explore her belief that each person is a product of what came before him and what is happening around him. She is very grateful to her loved ones for their continued support and willingness to see versions of themselves appear in her work.

Sarah Peden

What Does Not Change

There were ants on the poured concrete slab that day, the same as now, madly scurrying back and forth in their never-ceasing trek from hill to unknown destination and back again. I sat there, my little seven-year-old legs tucked up under me (just as they are now—some things never change). I squashed the odd ant that would stray too near me, not particularly desiring to have them climbing all over me.

Dad crouched nearby, a stringer of fish stretched on the grass before us that Saturday morning. He had his filet knife out and sharpened, for we had been up since dawn, just him and me, fishing the river that ran through our village about a mile from our house. I sat there squishing ants and watching my dad filet the fish. Looking back, I realize how unfazed I was by the process. You'd think a seven-year-old girl would be disgusted by the sight of fish guts, but I sat there calmly observing, fascinated even, as my dad pointed out the still beating heart, the liver and other organs. These he would later bag up and throw away or maybe bury somewhere so they could process back into the cycle of nature.

Those times were my times. Before brothers one through six were born, and grew old enough to handle the canoe and the fishing and before I began to cultivate a taste for indoor activities. Later I developed girly sensibilities and became squeamish around fish in their spasmodic floppy death throes.

I wonder if ants stick to a specific region forever. Are those ants still there on the stoop of the little white Cape Cod in Bald-winsville? Or, at least, are the great-grandchildren there? These ants have been here all day. Three times today at various hours I have crossed this sidewalk, and each time the ants were there, streaming back and forth. They go along their way, tugging at bits of sweet dried grass thrown up on the path by the mowers, always bumping into each other in passing. The day goes on, but they're still there.

In the bottom drawer of his dresser, my dad has a stack of newspapers, nine of them, ranging from 1991 to 2008. There's one for each child, picked up on the day we were born. On my twenty-first birthday Dad brought mine to my room, after cake was eaten, dinner cleaned up, and friends gone home.

"I thought you might like to see this," he said handing it to me.

I spread it out on the floor, flipping through the discolored pages. An article about Lea Salonga caught my eye. I had just learned about her vocal role in one of my favorite Disney mov-ies from a friend at school. That was the only printed story that interested me, but tucked between the folds of the newsprint lay a length of paper from an old dot-matrix printer, its perforated feed tracks still intact. I gently unfolded the half dozen sheets to find a homemade banner, ink faded to grey, proclaiming, *Welcome Home Baby Peden!* with two pixilated clip-art babies on either end of the text. I called my dad back to see this little relic of my past. Either his coworkers or my grandfather was my dad's guess on the origin of the banner, but he couldn't remember for sure.

My hunch was that my grandfather was the source. As long as I've known him, he's always had the newest technologi-cal gadget, so him having a printer back in 1991 was plausible. I remember when we got a dot matrix printer in our own house. We were living in the house of the early morning fishing trips. There were only four of us kids at the time. I didn't understand anything about the computer or the printer and how they worked;

though, later, I would hang around and learn bits and pieces from my dad—just enough to make me dangerous. I loved the special paper with its removable feed tracks. There's something extremely satisfying about tearing a perfectly perforated line.

Our computers evolved over the years, games on DOS-based shareware were upgraded when we got a CD-ROM drive. We got Internet for the first time; we got speakers. There were always the hand-me-down towers that would eventually wear out. Every time a computer was taken apart for upgrades, I was there at my dad's elbow, watching, fascinated as he operated on the guts of the machinery. Even these days, I'm still right there when something goes wrong on the home network, watching him tinker with IP addresses and subnet gateways, till the family's four computers are running online again in some sense of technological harmony. The machines we have running now are very different from the ancient setup we had when I was eight, but the fascination for technology remains alongside the respect I have for my dad's expertise. Mom says he's my biggest fan. I believe it. But he may not know that I'm his biggest fan, as only the first-born can be.

Thanksgiving approaches, and corporate worship chapels are filled with songs of gratitude: "Great is thy faithfulness, O God my Father. There is no shadow of turning with thee."

I think of my dad. Despite the fact that I've grown up and out of fishing trips, and contrasted against the many things that change—become "new and improved"—overnight, he's still there, the same old loving dad. How much greater then is my Father who "changeth not," and whose "compassions, they fail not."

As he was there from the beginning, he will still be forever.

I go home occasionally during the school year, and my dad still goes on fishing trips with my brothers, though maybe not as frequently. They will wake up before dawn or perhaps go out in the dead of night to float the river. But on the last Saturday of my visits home, we get up before breakfast, just him and me, and we drive down to our favorite coffee shop. These times are my times, when I remember again my birth order.

There in the coffee shop, as on the solitude of the river, there's no one but the two of us in anonymity. We share these moments with nothing profound being said, but it's comforting to know that, some things never change.

Maybe the ants will still be here tomorrow, I don't know. Maybe they will have been uprooted and moved on. But I know that somewhere on this earth, ants will still be there, making that never tiring trek from hill to who knows where.

 **Sarah Peden** is a student at Bryan College where she is pursuing her "choose-your-own-adventure" (liberal arts) major with hopes of graduate school and a masters in library science in the future. When she is not organizing children's books for her library internship, you can often find her drinking tea and blogging in the dorm.

Sarah loves finding beauty in the ordinary and cultivating the relationships that enrich her life. Be it friends or family, she draws inspiration from the people around her and writes out of the experiences that she has as she learns the art of living well.

L. M.

Down the Hill from Here

The campsite to which Edgar fled in the early evening of April 12th wasn't what he would call nature, but it was close to his apartment or what once was his apartment. Right outside of Yeaddiss, the fifteen-acre site sat off and below a curving paved road where campers could hear semis ferrying coal and gasoline rumble up and down throughout the night.

Inside the dark and dank campground rec room, the blinds half-drawn and lined with angels of dust, Edgar pressed his hand into the cushion of a graying couch and heard the springs creak in rust, smelt mildew release from its fabric.

"Feel free to plug in any of these games and give them a spin. I tested em out last week. Excepting the Space Invaders, they all work just fine."

The voice echoed out from a corner of the room. An old man with one shoulder slouched lower than the other wiped his glasses on a button-down shirt as red as the mayhaw jam Edgar once bought on a trip through Houma, LA. The old man leaned over a half-wet mop, sweeping a circle of dust over and over.

Edgar nodded at the old man and tapped his finger on the glass top of a large hulking machine, turning its ashy knobs. The remainders of past intergalactic wars had burnt faint shadows of spaceships and meteors onto the screen.

"Did Cheryl already get you set up with a site?"

"She did."

The man, spindly, raw, broken in, worn out, his legs and torso as long as a birch, propped the mop against the wall and sat down on the couch. He had no fear of its grime, sat on it every night at about this time to have some peace.

"I've never seen you in town before," Edgar said.

"You're from here," the man said.

"I live over in Cutshin." Edgar sat down in a moth-eaten chair facing the couch.

Ignoring him, the man said, "You should go and get your tent set up before dark. Otherwise it's a real bitch."

Edgar watched the old man stare at a television set that wasn't turned on. Above the TV was a small window that allowed a stream of light to funnel into the room, and on the gray screen Edgar could see both of their reflections. The bags under the old man's eyes mimicked the drooping lobes of his ears. His face was unshaven and unclean. There was probably no one to stay fresh for. Edgar guessed he'd probably look like the man if he stayed around long enough.

#

The sky had grown black and heavy with clouds. Edgar sat on the edge of a fire and looked up but couldn't see the stars. The wood near the toes of his boots crackled like glass in a chandelier, although society's hum was far far from here.

He licked his lips, tasting the sting of soot and juice of a Hebrew National hot dog from a pack he'd taken from the fridge and thrown into his bag along with his other stuff. Lyla had told him to pack his things—because this was the last time she was having a delinquent boyfriend ever again—and then kicked his duffel with her bare foot, causing her big toenail to bleed, so she was both screaming and crying at him at the same time. Into the duffel, he'd thrown in a couple pairs of jeans, his father's old Levi's jacket, a pair of orange socks from his sister Kimberly, a toothbrush, a photo of the family dog, a map of Canada with the camp-sites his cousin and he had stayed at marked in red sharpie, rolled up and secured with a rubber band, a can opener. He wasn't sure when he'd be back.

The wind kicked up, and he stirred the ashes with the heel of his boot. He pulled his Pendleton on over his head.

Back at home Lyla was probably curled up in their bed watching a sitcom. She kept up with five or six of the most popular shows for her job, so that when someone came in and sat in the dentist's chair and started blabbing about what Tricia did to Jake on that one sitcom, Lyla and her patient had something to relate about. It mattered to her to fit in here, and she did. She wasn't born in Yeaddiss like he was but in the town next door, Cutshin, where they both now lived. She was eight years younger than him, and her entire life had been in Cutshin. Yeaddiss had burned before she was born.

He got up and walked over to the edge of a stream flowing behind the site, dipping the lip of a plastic gallon into it and allow-ing its gentle current to bring water into the basin. Over the fire he dumped the water. The last embers hissed at him before going quiet. He crawled into the tent and fell asleep with his clothes on.

He woke up shivering. His chest was sticky and cold, and his sleeping bag was scrunched up at the base of the tent. The air inside was musky, unexposed to any oxygen since last fall's cam-pouts. As he knelt to button up his shirt, the sunlight cast his shadow against the opposite panel, one person and the illusion of another. He pulled on his jeans and got into the truck.

The road wound out of the campsite like a snake, follow-ing the natural undulations of the earth in its mountains and runs. Sometimes he felt like taking the road on out past the mountains, to keep going as far as he could. People always told him that he looked like a model, that he could use his looks to get somewhere better. But how did they know what it would take to get out of here, to New York or Los Angeles or even Nashville? He had been to these cities, seen the types of men and the types of things they could buy with their money. Washington, Memphis, San Francisco, New Orleans, he'd seen them all and wasn't too fond of the endless buzzing and beeping, the lights that never seemed to go dim. He had no misconceptions about what it took to make it out there.

The wind licked his hair out from beneath his baseball cap, the tendrils soft as that of a younger man. He held the wheel between his knees, grasping his cap with one hand and smoothed his hair back down with the other. He was too old to try to become something else.

As the truck came down the hill Edgar felt the sun easing off again, clouds dabbing the sky. Nothing like that Appalachian weather. Nothing like it in the world.

The backseat of his truck was filled with government pamphlets reminding locals to throw away their trash in the proper receptacles, to recycle their beer bottles, soda cans, two liters, to scoop their pets' feces (to prevent harmful runoff). The Department of Environmental Resources was headquartered in a former one-room schoolhouse from the frontier era that somebody thought to convert into an office. Every day from eight to four Edgar sat at one of the three metal desks alongside his supervisor Alvin and the secretary Cathy. There was a small TV in the office that they left running most of the day. On his salary, he could pay his and Lyla's rent, eat out from time to time, go on trips to Montana or the Adirondacks.

He took a pack of cigarettes from the glove compartment, tucked them into his shirt pocket and grabbed his backpack with his equipment and his camera. He shut the car door and began the walk uphill.

The threat of sinkholes frightened no one. Tourists and locals alike ignored the chain that blocked the road up to the mine, ostensibly barring entrants from pursuing their curiosities. Officials (himself included) said there was still a threat, the underground coal fires still raging after twenty-four years. They had managed to scare most of the residents away. But the people left in Yeaddiss said that the fires had migrated east, away from town. They said its noxious gases were long gone, the quality of the air just fine; you could tell by breathing it. No one had fallen into a sinkhole in over twenty years. A young boy and his dog. They did disappear. But that was a long time ago.

On the edge of a small drop-off he noticed a smoking perforation in the dusty ground. He removed a thermometer, a string tied to its end, and lowered it down into the hole. From his backpack he took out his camera, pointed it at the hole, the lens fogging up, and released the shutter.

He thought of Eleanor Crowley and Lawrence Crowley and Patrick Beyer who all still lived here. Eleanor and Lawrence, sixty-eight years old, were twins and lived in the same house. Patrick was Edgar's cousin.

The outlines of the mountains in the distance rose up out of the cresting fog. He knelt down and pressed his palm to the earth. The dry ground held a residual warmth, the vestigial heat of a body attending death. Edgar lowered his head to the ground, his ear flat to the dust, listening for the soft murmurs of subterranean wind currents. He got up from the ground and continued the trek upwards, the sun trying to peek out.

\#

At the top of the hill where the land began to flatten out stood a lone house, tall and reaching and awkward. Once the middle unit in a three-home rowhouse, the government had bulldozed the two adjoining homes when their inhabitants left town. To keep the middle house from falling over, Patrick and a few workers had installed long titanium poles at the four corners of the foundation. Even with the poles the house leaned noticeably to the left, a sizable sinkhole sucking part of the porch into the earth.

Edgar stopped in front of the lolling structure and pulled his shirt up over his nose. A haze of putrid air cloaked Patrick's property because he burned all of his trash in the backyard, old food, cans, plastic packaging, whatever. The garbage men didn't come out here anymore. He walked up the steps and gave a warning knock.

"Eating," Patrick called back from inside the house.

Edgar walked into the kitchen, its wood floors, wood cabinets, and Formica countertops all layered in a thin film of dust, the walls a robin's egg blue. In the middle of the room, Patrick sat at a desk, a long oblong thing that looked to be the quality of balsa wood.

"Nice desk. Is that an Ikea?" Edgar went to the fridge and pulled out one of five plastic jugs of water. The groundwater had been contaminated by coal waste. Mostly arsenic and lead. A little bit of cadmium and selenium. Edgar took a red plastic cup from a stack on the counter and sat down on the other side of the desk.

"The legs on Mom's table gave out with The Sinkhole. Found this desk out on 699." The Sinkhole referred not to the one that took out the porch, but the one that took out the core of the house. It had carved a giant hole into the center of the living room and took an old rug and a coffee table but managed to leave the TV.

"Why don't you get someone to do something about the hole?" Edgar filled the cup to the top, drank it in one gulp, then filled another.

"Too expensive." Patrick licked the grease from his fingers. "And it doesn't bother me too much. I just sit on the other side of the room from it. Don't think about it."

Edgar stood up and threw the plastic cup into a large gray outdoor garbage bin. All of Patrick's plates and cups were plastic. A peremptory measure, Edgar guessed.

"It's too quiet in this house is the problem. I'm getting tired of it."

He had never heard Patrick admit to the loneliness that everyone in the family and in Cutshin knew that people in Yeaddiss must feel. There was no way a man could live by himself with a pit peeking down to hell giving him a daily reminder of his mortality. It was too much, they said. Too much.

"I need someone in here. Maybe a subletter, so in case it doesn't work out I can just switch him out for another." He rubbed his eyes hard with the insides of his wrists and tucked his hands into his armpits, leaning back. "What do you think?"

"You could ask Daisy."

"My sister's not living here again. Tried that. Too many boyfriends coming in and out of here."

"Put up an ad in Cutshin."

"This goddamn thing keeps beeping. Beep Beep! Beep yourself!" Patrick banged his fist against a small off-white box on the wall. "It's always beeping."

"I can take a look at that for you."

"You know I don't go into town. And besides, anyone in town won't want to live here. They won't like the holes." When they deemed Yeaddiss unlivable, most residents moved over to Cutshin. Patrick held a grudge against his former townspeople, who he thought had given up on an idyllic place. He drove to a town forty miles away to get groceries.

Edgar leaned forward, placing his forehead on the desk. He could make out the faint sound of the fire thirty or forty feet down through the thin table and the floorboards and the grass and the topsoil. This time, the wind was louder. Maybe not wind at all. A hush.

Edgar said, "Well I'll keep an eye out for any wayward Chicagoans who need a place to stay and send them your way. Hotel Beyer."

Patrick got up from the table and went to the tap. He cupped his hands and allowed the slow drip of the faucet to pool before dipping his face and holding it there. Edgar could hear the bubbles forming as Patrick breathed in and out.

He resurfaced and said, "That other bedroom isn't getting any use now. Use it anytime you want." He walked out of the kitchen and into the family room. Patrick dug his hands into his pockets, an index finger poking out through a raggedy hole, and stared down into The Sinkhole. He took a cigar from his back pocket, already cut, and lit it, rolling the smoke around inside his bony cheeks, as thin and webby as moth-eaten sheets.

Edgar walked up next to him and took out a cigarette. They had spent a lot of time together. One night when they were camping down near the Grand Canyon, a rattlesnake had found its way inside Edgar's sleeping bag, burrowed itself down by his feet. Patrick skewered the thing right through with his pocket knife. And on their trip to Memphis, Edgar paid for gas both there and back because he knew Patrick didn't have the money. They trusted each other in a way that only comes after years of shared mundane and extraordinary experiences.

Edgar smoked cigarettes until Patrick's cigar whittled down to the tip of a thumb.

"I gotta get going soon, but I'll come by sometime next week to make sure you're still breathing," Edgar said, slapping his cousin on the back. Patrick's torso swayed slightly, but his feet stayed planted, and he gave him a laugh.

#

He heard her car coming from five minutes down the road. He waited for her to pull up, the gravel shifting beneath her braking tires, before moving down from the porch.

"You don't have to come in. I know you don't like coming here."

"Oh cut the crap," she said, cranking the handle to close her window. He opened the door for her. Her A-line skirt fell in folds as she swung her legs out of the car.

"Why are you dressed up so nice?"

"My parents are having a going away party for me tonight." She had gotten engaged to a man from Pittsburgh and was moving away. "I gotta run in a sec. But I was packing up the apartment and found your radio. Thought you might want this, for all the entertaining you two do over here." She reached into the passenger seat, giving him a glimpse of her lower back as her thin shirt rode up.

"Have you even been out here before?"

"Of course I've been here." She extended her hands holding the radio. "I'd go and watch the boys ride motorcross out on the highway. You never did that though. You didn't like motorbikes."

"No, I didn't care much about motorbikes."

She cleared her throat and spit into the grass. She managed to look pretty doing it. The apples in her cheeks glowed with a soft red hue. He couldn't help that he still found her attractive. She'd get more looks where she was going, and he wasn't sure she'd know how to deal with it. Big city life.

"Thanks for dropping this by."

"You really want to stay here?"

"Yeah, I do."

"You know you could have stayed in our place for a month or so longer. Until you got it together."

"It was better for me to get out. But thanks."

"It's a shithole, Ed."

"It's pretty fine."

"There are holes everywhere. You could fall in when you two are stumbling around drunk or a new hole could suck you up while you're sleeping."

"I don't drink that much." Which was true, but he only said "I" because Patrick was drunk pretty regularly.

She took a step back from him and crossed her arms over her chest. "Tell Patrick I say ahoy hoy sailor boy," she said, letting a smile crack her serious expression. It was some joke the two of them shared. Patrick was always watching movies about sea-faring folk and their women and gold and sunsets.

She walked back to her car and opened the door, her hand gripping the metal. She was ready to go, and she didn't understand what was left in this place for anyone. This was no place to have a life.

He gave her a nod and waved, returning a look that was more confident, he thought, than hers.

The sun fell behind the mountains. Edgar sipped a beer, perspiration soaking into his hand, and stared out at what lay before him. He and Patrick could make a life of their own out here. Maybe go to Cutshin and find two nice girls to bring back. Life was like that. You never knew what could happen.

Down the hill from here, a yellow and orange plastic jungle gym once stood. Now half-melted into the earth, its four legs plastered down in an eternal state of drip, a sea monster whose feet were forever tangled in a cretaceous morass. He thought of the hundreds, certainly not thousands, of children who had climbed up the rungs of its ladder, who had dirtied their trousers on its rain and mud soaked slide. He liked to think about the jungle gym as it once was, a thing where children and their families played and laughed and flourished.

But it was something different now. Its state of melted disuse reminded him of the conch shells that littered the Caribbean beaches of Patrick's movies: hollowed out, discarded, the remainders of something once breathing. Looking at the jungle gym now was like when those pirates got old and returned forever to England or France or North Carolina, wherever they were from, and held that shell to their ear, knowing that the real ocean is far far away. They kept that shell on their dresser and looked at it from time to time. Sometimes the seashell is good enough. Sometimes it's all you need.

 **L. M.** was born and raised in Virginia. Her writings have earned her attendance to the Sewanee Writers' Conference, a University Award for Projects in the Arts from the University of Virginia, and publication in the *Eunoia Review* and the *Stoneslide Corrective*. She currently resides in New Orleans.

Michael Brown

Without

Without _____, the sun   shines
Too brigh
tly
Without_____, the cold does
Not   matter.
I don't need a coat.

Without _____, I   don't want
To smile
Without _____, I can   not
Laugh

Without _____ there, other   people
Are just   blurs.
Without _____, life has
No
Reason
No rh
Thym
No rhyme
Love _____.

Absurdist Delight

GIRL: A girl.
BOY: A boy.
SETTING: Somewhere. Some time. There is a bench.

(GIRL sits by BOY. BOY looks empty.)

GIRL: Why would you say that?
BOY: Say what?
GIRL: What you said.
BOY: What did I say?

(GIRL looks away.)

GIRL: You know what you said.
    (Pause.)

BOY: Yeah. I know.
    (Pause.)

GIRL: So why would you say that?
BOY: Why wouldn't I?
GIRL: I understand.
BOY: I know you do.
    (Beat.)

(BOY sits down on the ground.)

BOY: I understand.
GIRL: Do you?
BOY: I think I do.
GIRL: I'm sorry.
BOY: I'm sorry.
    (Beat.)

GIRL: Are you?
BOY: Am I?

(GIRL sits by BOY.)

GIRL: You are.
BOY: I am.
    (Pause.)

BOY: I want to say something.
GIRL: What?
BOY: You know.
GIRL: Do I?

(BOY puts his knees up. Rests his arms on his knees. Hangs his head.)

BOY: I hope you do.

Abraham Lincoln, Racist Hunter

It is 3:47 am. I cannot sleep tonight…this morning…whatever. It's because I have a lot on my mind, but there is one thought. One thought that infectiously invades every crevice of my brain.

Today…yesterday…whatever, I read that the KKK was coming to visit a town close by. You figure racism would be blighted enough to not be able to support a group like that, at least, not here in America. ('Merica as some may say.) But whatever. I have to remind myself that this is the South. And while the South has many things that are good: the rich molasses sounds of a Savannah accent, fried chicken, Julia Roberts (she's from Georgia…unless Wikipedia is lying again), I have to remember that the South is the finest example of time travel. When the world moves forward, the South decides to go back, back to the past. Where racism is alive.

And that's where I begin to fantasize. I think about it. Growing out my beard (which is red) and dyeing it a dark color. Slicking back my hair. I think about chopping down a tree. And making from this tree the finest baseball bat the world has seen. I put on the suit. The dark suit. I put on a dark, long hat. Before you know it (a la Seth Grahame-Smith) I become ABRAHAM LINCOLN, RACIST HUNTER.

Armed with my bat, the North American Avenger of Colored People. I go to the rally. I unplug their microphones. I use my own. I say:

"Four days and seven shots of scotch ago, I grew a beard. Or maybe that was four weeks ago…whatever. Anyway, I decided to crash your party to…tell you to get out of here! Yeah, get out of here!

Now we are engaged in a very awkward moment, testing my alcohol tolerance and testing your patience for a fake Abraham Lincoln. We are met…we are met? Is that even proper English?"

92

At this point, I vomit from nervousness and the aforementioned seven shots of scotch. Lucky for me, the robes are very absorbent. I leap into the crowd, swinging my baseball bat. They are caught unawares. They fall under the fury of my bat, my Baseball Bat of Multiracial Justice. But they fight back. I fall under the Fatal Fist of Racist Injustice. Lost all seems….

But then a man wearing a Barack Obama mask crashes through the White Curtain of Ignorance. He comes to my side.

"Who…who are you?" I ask him. He only extends his hand and picks me up from the ground. As I stand, a man with a Freddie Mercury-esque moustache breaks through the Crowd of White Supremacy. "And who are you?" I ask. He opens his mouth. He gives no answer but instead, sings a note of the Heavens.

Then it dawns on me. These are no imposters. This is Barack Obama. This is Freddie Mercury.

And as I prepare to leap back into the fray, I feel a hand on my shoulder. It is Abraham Lincoln. I meet his eyes; he says, "Go, my son."

Barack, Freddie, and I rush forward. Racism and homophobia crumbling before our might. No hope for the Klan. The ground suddenly splits open.

"Klansmen! Retreat!" shouts their leader. "This isn't over RACIST HUNTER!"

The ground closes. My beard is gone. I look to Freddie. He nods and sings, returning to Heaven to sing God a lullaby. Barack nods and flies off. Apparently, that is a side-effect of the Presidency. Lincoln's spirit is also gone.

I return to my apartment and collapse on my couch. I look to my left, and there stands Lincoln.

"Lincoln! What are you doing here?" I ask.

"I need a place to crash." He answered.

But this is all a fantasy. It is now 4:44 am, and I have finished my story…fantasy…. Whatever.

 **Michael Brown** is a theatre major at Young Harris College and a native of Georgia. He shares a passion for acting and writing and enjoys talking to friends and family about ideas to improve the worlds of acting and writing. Michael would like to go on to use his writing as a means to not only entertain and inspire others, but to support his loving and always supportive parents. Having a vivid and fun imagination, Michael uses his theatre training to improve upon his ideas to provide the best experience for the reader.

Michael wishes to thank all the readers, his editor, friends and family for their support.

Critical Reading Questions and Writing Exercises

These critical reading questions and writing exercises are designed to enable young readers to engage with and explore the literature of the young writers of this anthology. Each question or exercise includes a reference to one or more of the Common Core State Standards with which it aligns. A listing of those standards is included at the end of this section for reference purposes.

"The Fish"

1. How would you describe the relationship between the narrator and her father? Cite details from the text to support your answer.
[CCSS-ELA-Literacy.RL.9-10.1, 11-12.1; W.9-10-1, 11-12.1]

2. Write a poem or short story that provides insight into aspects of a relationship you have with another person.
[CCSS-ELA-Literarcy.W.9-10.3, 11-12.3]

"Dying Language"

1. How does the narrator perceive gender and age affecting her experiences? Cite details from the poem to support your claim.
[CCSS-ELA-Literacy.RL.9-10.2, 11-12.2]

2. Write a letter or a poem to someone who is different from you in some aspect: gender, age, ethnicity, etc. Attempt to explain to them ways in which you see the world differently than he or she does.
[CCSS-ELA-Literarcy.W.9-10.4, 11-12.4]

"I Share Your Harvest"

1. How do the central agrarian terms, phrases and metaphors contribute to the meaning of the poem? Cite details from the poem.
[CCSS-ELA-Literacy.RL.9-10.4, 11-12.4]
2. Write a brief explanation of how images of growing plants are used to convey meaning. Use an example from this poem or another story you have read to illustrate your point.
[CCSS-ELA-Literarcy.W.9-10.2, 11-12.2]

"Peter, Beloved"

1. How does the author's decision to refer to the adult characters only using titles (mother, father) but to use names for the children contribute to the tensions within the story?
[CCSS-ELA-Literacy.RL.9-10.5, 11-12.5]
2. "In the absence of a name, we perceive of someone as less than fully human." Write a brief essay in which you state why you agree or disagree. Include analysis from the story to bolster your position.
[CCSS-ELA-Literarcy.W.9-10.1, 11-12.1, RL.9-10.1, 11-12.1]

"Paper-Nymphs"

1. What is the narrator saying about her internal state of mind? Her interactions with others? Cite details from the poem to support your analysis.
[CCSS-ELA-Literacy.RL.9-10.2, 11-12.2]
2. Describe a habit that you have like doodling absentmindedly. Explain what you believe that reveals about you as a person.
[CCSS-ELA-Literarcy.W.9-10.2, 11-12.2]

"City Streets"

1. What is does the word "wheel" and the use of color words contribute to the meaning of the poem?
[CCSS-ELA-Literacy.RL.9-10.4, 11-12.4]
2. Think of a scene, such as a city street, and then focus in on one specific element that is common to that scene. Use that one element to fully describe the scene.
[CCSS-ELA-Literarcy.W.9-10.3, 11-12.3]

"Red Yellow Blue"

1. How does the narrator see herself as a character who has developed over time? Cite details from the poem to support your analysis.
[CCSS-ELA-Literacy.RL.9-10.1, 9-10.3, 11-12.1, 11-12.3]
2. Write a letter or a poem to someone you know well. Describe how you perceive your development as a person. Show how experiences in the past contributed to you becoming the person you are now.
[CCSS-ELA-Literarcy.W.9-10.4, 11-12.4]

"Bathtub"

1. How does the narrator's description of entering a bathtub parallel other experiences or events in life?
[CCSS-ELA-Literacy.RL.9-10.2, 11-12.2]
2. Think of something you do everyday. Write a poem or essay that explains all the little details involved in doing that thing.
[CCSS-ELA-Literarcy.W.9-10.2, 11-12.2]

"The Immortal Dreams"

1. How does the contrast in the lines that begin with "I fish my dreams" and end with a specific location create a sense of surprise and contribute to the meaning of the poem?
[CCSS-ELA-Literacy.RL.9-10.4, 9-10.5, 11-12.4, 11-12.5]

2. Choose one of the stanzas from the poem. Analyze the meaning of "I fish my dreams" within that specific stanza. Cite details from the poem.
[CCSS-ELA-Literarcy.W.9-10.1, 11-12.1]

"Love Prayers"

1. How is the poet connecting the image of a bird and the image of a mother in the poem? How does that tie into the central idea? Cite details from the poem to support your claim.
[CCSS-ELA-Literacy.RL.9-10.2 11-12.2]

2. Write a poem that is draws a comparison between two different images. Show how both images can illustrate the same main idea.
[CCSS-ELA-Literarcy.W.9-10.3, 11-12.3]

"Fantasy"

1. The sense of sound and hearing is central to the poem. How do the different types of hearing contribute to the development of the poem? Cite details from the poem.
[CCSS-ELA-Literacy.RL.9-10.1, 9-10.4, 11-12.1, 11-12.4]

2. Choose a sense other than the sense of sight. Write a poem in which you only use images related to that one sense.
[CCSS-ELA-Literarcy.W.9-10.3, 11-12.3]

"Memory Lane"

1. How does the repetition of the first and last stanza affect the meaning of the poem?
[CCSS-ELA-Literacy.RL.9-10.1, 9-10.4, 11-12.1, 11-12.4]

2. Think about the way songs will repeat a chorus several times. Write an explanation as to what that accomplishes and why that is an effective technique.
[CCSS-ELA-Literarcy.W.9-10.2, 11-12.2]

"Hi Jaw-jaw"

1. How does the relationship between the narrator and Jimmy change over the course of the story? Cite details to support your analysis.
[CCSS-ELA-Literacy.RL.9-10.3, 9-10.1, 11-12.3, 11-12.1]

2. Write a letter or poem to someone you have known for several years. Describe an event that changed your perception of them. Explain how your relationship changed because of what occurred.
[CCSS-ELA-Literarcy.W.9-10.4, 11-12.4]

"Afternoon Lullaby"

1. How does the image of the mother and child morph over the course of the story? What does this communicate about the relationship between the various characters in the poem?
[CCSS-ELA-Literacy.RL.9-10.3, 11-12.3]

2. Write a brief essay that explains how you have perceived your relationship to other people change as you have grown older and a new insight maturity has given you.
[CCSS-ELA-Literarcy.W.9-10.2, 11-12.2]

"Point Pleasant Beach in January"

1. What aspects of the sea gull contrast with the narrator's perception of herself and her life? Cite details from the poem to support your claim.
[CCSS-ELA-Literacy.RL.9-10.2, 11-12.2]

2. Write a brief essay that explains the connection between the narrator's trouble forgetting herself and the final line of the poem. Cite details from the poem.
[CCSS-ELA-Literarcy.W.9-10.2, 11-12.2]

"Anniversary Card: To My Mother"

1. What details about the relationship between the father and the mother are revealed by the father's interaction with the narrator?
[CCSS-ELA-Literacy.RL.9-10.3, 11-12.3]

2. "The Child is father of the Man." Analyze the central idea of the poem and discuss how it compares and contrasts to this quote.
[CCSS-ELA-Literarcy.W.9-10.1, 11-12.1]

"My Grandmother Marie"

1. What parallels does the poem draw between the grandmother and the narrator?
[CCSS-ELA-Literacy.RL.9-10.3, 11-12.3]

2. Write a letter or a poem to someone close to you. Explain how shared experiences have created significant connections between the two of you.
[CCSS-ELA-Literarcy.W.9-10.4, 11-12.4]

"Twenty-Nine Days More"

1. What does the poem reveal about the two levels of consciousness in which the narrator is operating? Cite details from the poem to support your analysis
[CCSS-ELA-Literacy.RL.9-10.1, 11-12.1]

2. Write a poem or a short story about a character in a coffee shop that contrasts the outward experience with the inward experience of the character.
[CCSS-ELA-Literarcy.W.9-10.3, 11-12.3]

"Sunday"

1. How does the narrator convey the central tension of the poem? Cite examples from the poem to support your position.
[CCSS-ELA-Literacy.RL.9-10.5, 11-12.5]

2. Write a letter or poem to someone you have felt anger towards. Explain how your anger affected the relationship between the two of you.
[CCSS-ELA-Literarcy.W.9-10.4, 11-12.4]

"Junkyard"

1. What is the connection between the brother and the junkyard-related words and images in the poem? Cite details from the poem to support your analysis.
[CCSS-ELA-Literacy.RL.9-10.1, 9-10.4, 11-12.1, 11-12.4]

2. Explain what the poem reveals about the relationship between the narrator and her brother. Provide specific examples from the poem.
[CCSS-ELA-Literarcy.W.9-10.1, 9-10.2, 11-12.1, 11-12.2]

"What Does Not Change"

1. What do the ants reveal about the narrator's perception of the relationship between her and her father? Cite specific details from the story to support your analysis.
[CCSS-ELA-Literacy.RL.9-10.1, 9-10.3, 11-12.1, 11-12.3]

2. Write a short story or play that captures an aspect of your experience as a young child growing up and embodies that experience in a symbol.
[CCSS-ELA-Literarcy.W.9-10.3, 11-12.3]

"Down the Hill from Here"

1. How does the contrast between Edgar's relationship with Lyla versus his relationship with Patrick connect to the theme of the story?
[CCSS-ELA-Literacy.RL.9-10.2, 9-10.3, 11-12.2, 11-12.3]

2. Write an essay that explains the connection between the melted jungle gym and Edgar's situation. Cite specific details from the story to support your analysis.
[CCSS-ELA-Literarcy.W.9-10.1, 9-10.2, 11-12.1, 11-12.2]

"Without"

1. How does the repetition of an explicitly missing word expand the possible meanings of the poem?
[CCSS-ELA-Literacy.RL.9-10.4, 11-12.4]

2. Choose a verb, adjective or adverb. Then write a poem in which you repeatedly omit a word corresponding to that part of speech.
[CCSS-ELA-Literarcy.W.9-10.3, 11-12.3]

"Absurdist Delight"

1. What does this play reveal about the challenges of inter-personal communication?
[CCSS-ELA-Literacy.RL.9-10.2, 11-12.2]

2. 'By the end of the play the girl and the boy have managed to understand with each other.' Explain whether or not you think that statement is true. Cite details from the play that support your analysis.
[CCSS-ELA-Literarcy.W.9-10.2, 9-10.1, 11-12.2, 11-12.1]

"Abraham Lincoln, Racist Hunter"

1. What does the appearance of each historical figure reveal about the narrator's perception of himself? Cite details from the story to support your analysis.
[CCSS-ELA-Literacy.RL.9-10.1, 11-12.1]

2. Choose a historical figure with whom you identify. Write a letter to that person. Persuade that person to join you in addressing a specific social issue. Describe how that person could help you achieve a solution to the problem.
[CCSS-ELA-Literarcy.W.9-10.4, 11-12.4]

Common Core State Standards, Reading: Literature

CCSS.ELA-Literacy.RL.9-10.1
Cite strong and thorough textual evidence to support analysis of what the text says explicitly as well as inferences drawn from the text.

CCSS.ELA-Literacy.RL.9-10.2
Determine a theme or central idea of a text and analyze in detail its development over the course of the text, including how it emerges and is shaped and refined by specific details; provide an objective summary of the text.

CCSS.ELA-Literacy.RL.9-10.3
Analyze how complex characters develop over the course of a text, interact with other characters, and advance the plot or develop the theme.

CCSS.ELA-Literacy.RL.9-10.4 Determine the meaning of words and phrases as they are used in the text, including figurative and connotative meanings; analyze the cumulative impact of specific word choices on meaning and tone.

CCSS.ELA-Literacy.RL.9-10.5 Analyze how an author's choices concerning how to structure a text, order events within it create such effects as mystery, tension, or surprise.

CCSS.ELA-Literacy.RL.9-10.6 Analyze a particular point of view or cultural experience reflected in a work of literature from outside the United States, drawing on a wide reading of world literature.

CCSS.ELA-Literacy.RL.11-12.1 Cite strong and thorough textual evidence to support analysis of what the text says explicitly as well as inferences drawn from the text, including determining where the text leaves matters uncertain.

CCSS.ELA-Literacy.RL.11-12.2 Determine two or more themes or central ideas of a text and analyze their development over the course of the text, including how they interact and build on one another to produce a complex account; provide an objective summary of the text.

CCSS.ELA-Literacy.RL.11-12.3 Analyze the impact of the author's choices regarding how to develop and relate elements of a story or drama.

CCSS.ELA-Literacy.RL.11-12.4 Determine the meaning of words and phrases as they are used in the text, including figurative and connotative meanings; analyze the impact of specific word choices on meaning and tone, including words with multiple meanings or language that is particularly fresh, engaging, or beautiful.

CCSS.ELA-Literacy.RL.11-12.5 Analyze how an author's choices concerning how to structure specific parts of a text contribute to its overall structure and meaning as well as its aesthetic impact.

CCSS.ELA-Literacy.RL.11-12.6 Analyze a case in which grasping a point of view requires distinguishing what is directly stated in a text from what is really meant.

Common Core State Standards, Writing

CCSS.ELA-Literacy.W.9-10.1 Write arguments to support claims in an analysis of substantive topics or texts, using valid reasoning and relevant and sufficient evidence.

CCSS.ELA-Literacy.W.9-10.2 Write informative/explanatory texts to examine and convey complex ideas, concepts, and information clearly and accurately through the effective selection, organization, and analysis of content.

CCSS.ELA-Literacy.W.9-10.3 Write narratives to develop real or imagined experiences or events using effective technique, well-chosen details, and well-structured event sequences.

CCSS.ELA-Literacy.W.9-10.4 Produce clear and coherent writing in which the development, organization, and style are appropriate to task, purpose, and audience.

CCSS.ELA-Literacy.W.11-12.1 Write arguments to support claims in an analysis of substantive topics or texts, using valid reasoning and relevant and sufficient evidence.

CCSS.ELA-Literacy.W.11-12.2 Write informative/explanatory texts to examine and convey complex ideas, concepts, and information clearly and accurately through the effective selection, organization, and analysis of content.

CCSS.ELA-Literacy.W.11-12.3 Write narratives to develop real or imagined experiences or events using effective technique, well-chosen details, and well-structured event sequences.

CCSS.ELA-Literacy.W.11-12.4 Produce clear and coherent writing in which the development, organization, and style are appropriate to task, purpose, and audience.

National Governors Association Center for Best Practices, Council of Chief State School Officers. *Common Core State Standards English Language Arts*. National Governors Association Center for Best Practices, Council of Chief State School Officers, Washington D.C. 2010

Permissions

Caroline DeLuca: "The Fish." Copyright 2013 by Caroline De-Luca. "Dying Language." Copyright 2013 by Caroline DeLuca. "I Share Your Harvest." Copyright 2013 by Caroline DeLuca. Printed by permission of the author.

Leah Gooodreau: "Peter, Beloved." Copyright © 2013 by Leah Goodreau. Printed by permission of the author.

Janelle Fine: "Paper-Nymphs." Copyright 2013 by Janelle Fine. "City Streets." Copyright 2013 by Janelle Fine. "Red Yellow Blue." Copyright 2013 by Janelle Fine. "Bathtub." Copyright 2013 by Janelle Fine. Printed by permission of the author.

Shefali Srivastava: "The Immortal Dreams." Copyright 2013 by Shefali Srivastava. "Love Prayers." Copyright 2013 by Shefali Srivastava. "Fantasy." Copyright 2013 by Shefali Srivastava. "Memory Lane." Copyright 2013 by Shefali Srivastava. Printed by permission of the author.

Georgia Googer: "Hi Jaw-jaw." Copyright 2012 by Georgia Googer. Printed by permission of the author.

Jolene Paternoster: "Afternoon Lullaby." Copyright 2012 by Jolene Paternoster. "Point Pleasant Beach in January." Copyright 2012 by Jolene Paternoster. "Anniversary Card: To My Mother." Copyright 2012 by Jolene Paternoster. "My Grandmother Marie." Copyright 2012 by Jolene Paternoster. "Twenty-Nine Days More." Copyright 2012 by Jolene Paternoster. "Sunday." Copyright 2012 by Jolene Paternoster. "Junkyard." Copyright 2012 by Jolene Paternoster. Printed by permission of the author.

Press

Empowering young writers to say, **"I am my scholarship!"**

Open call for submissions to the
Young Writers Anthology!

See your work in print!

Become a published writer!

**Earn royalites that can help
you pay for college!s**

VerbalEyze Press is accepting submissions from young adult writers,
ages 13 to 22, in any of the following genres:

- poetry
- short story
- songwriting
- playwriting
- graphic novel
- creative non-fiction

For submission details, visit
www.verbaleyze.org

VerbalEyze serves to foster, promote and support the development
and professional growth of emerging young writers.

Writers Cooperative

VerbalEyze is a nonprofit organization whose mission is to foster, promote and support the development and professional growth of emerging young writers.

The *Young Writers Anthology* is published as a service of VerbalEyze in furtherance of its goal to provide young writers with access to publishing opportunities that they otherwise would not have.

Fifty percent of the proceeds received from the sale of the *Young Writers Anthology* are paid to the authors in the form of scholarships to help them advance in their post-secondary education.

For more information about VerbalEyze and how you can become involved in its work with young writers, visit www.verbaleyze.org.